D1628010

Scholastic Publications Ltd
10 Earlham Street, London, WC2H 9RX, UK.

Scholastic Tab Publications Ltd
123 Newkirk Road, Richmond Hill,
Ontario, L4C 3G5, Canada.

Ashton Scholastic Pty Ltd
P O Box 579, Gosford, New South Wales,
Australia.

Ashton Scholastic Ltd
165 Marua Road, Panmure, Auckland 6,
New Zealand.

First published by Scholastic Publications Ltd., 1989.

Text © Hilary Whyard 1989

Illustrations © Hilary Whyard 1989

Oh No! Books © Culford Books 1989

Conceived, edited, designed and produced by
Culford Books, Sunningwell House, Sunningwell,
Abingdon, Oxfordshire, OX13 6RD

Editor Penelope Miller

House Designer Judith Allan

Cover Design Judith Allan

ISBN 0 590 76094 7

Photoset by Opus, Oxford

Printed and bound in Great Britain by
Purnell Book Production Ltd

10 9 8 7 6 5 4 3 2 1

For Linda and her very old bear.

Oh No!

Oliver Drops It

Hilary Whyard

Hippo Books
Scholastic Publications Limited
London

Oliver is Sam's teddy. He used to be Sam's mum's bear which means he is very old. Being old has not made Oliver at all sensible.

Here is what happened on the day Oliver and Sam decided to do some baking.

"Let's make jam tarts for everybody for tea," said Sam.

"Mix it up and make it nice.
'Pop' goes the weasel!"

"Here you are Oliver, you can play with this piece while I roll mine out."

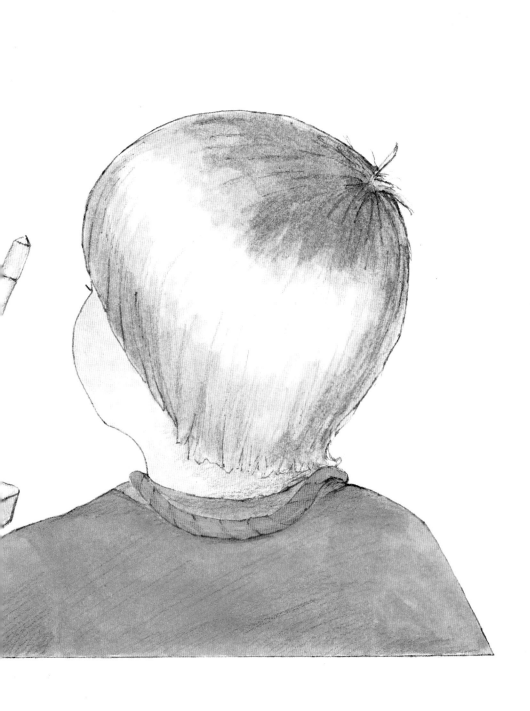

"What a lovely long snake, Oliver! I'm cutting mine into shapes now.

Oh, now it's a snail, that's clever. Here go my shapes into the tin.

Oh, poor snail, you've bashed him flat!

A spoonful of jam in this one, a spoonful of jam in that one . . ."

"That's a nice ball Oliver. Now, are you going to roll it out to make some tarts?"

"Oh no!" groaned Sam. "Oliver, don't throw it!"

"Oliver! You've dropped your pastry!"

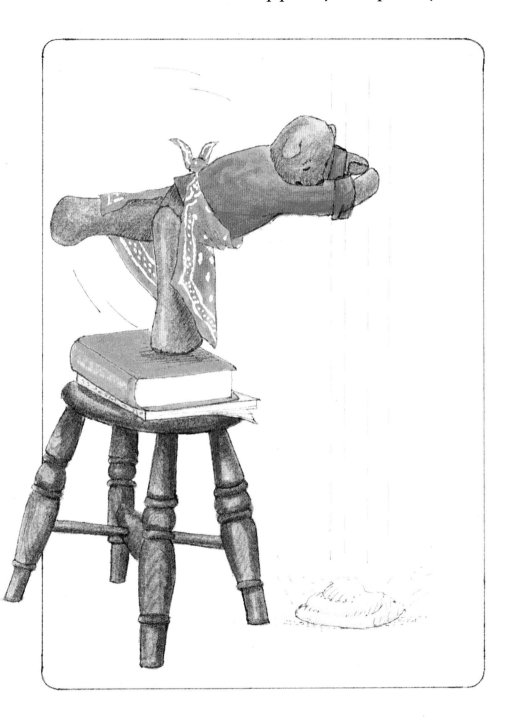

"And look at it –
all dirty and
hairy!

You can't make tarts
with it now."

"Oh, cheer up Oliver, you didn't mean to drop it, did you?
I've just thought of a special thing to do with it."

"If we tie a piece of
string around your
pastry . . ."

". . . we can hang it in the tree for the birds.
They can peck round
the dirty bits."

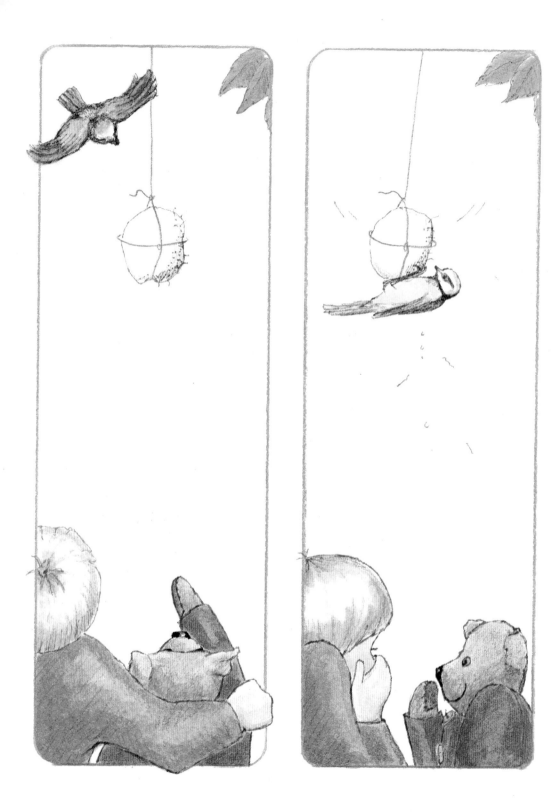

Soon the tree was full of birds
enjoying Oliver's pastry.

At morning snack time Sam shared
his tarts with Oliver.

At tea time they shared them with everyone.

And there were still two left over for the next day.

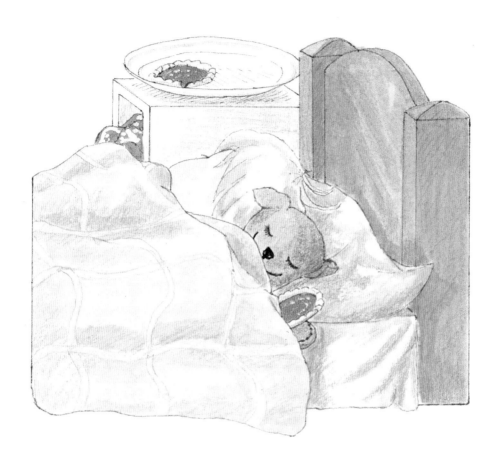

"Goodnight, Sam!"
"Goodnight, Oliver!"

Goodnight!